The GROSS AND GOOFY Body

Blasts of Gas

The Secrets of Breathing, Burping, and Passing Gas

By Melissa Stewart

Illustrated by Janet Hamlin

Marshall Cavendish
Benchmark
New York

This book was made possible,
in part, by a grant from the
Society of Children's Book Writers and Illustrators.

Marshall Cavendish Benchmark
99 White Plains Road
Tarrytown, NY 10591-5502
www.marshallcavendish.us

Library of Congress Cataloging-in-Publication Data
Stewart, Melissa.
Blasts of gas : the secrets of breathing, burping, and passing gas / by
Melissa Stewart.
p. cm. — (The gross and goofy body)
Includes index.
Summary: "Provides comprehensive information on the role gas plays in the
body science of humans and animals"—Provided by publisher.
ISBN 978-0-7614-4155-7
1. Respiration—Juvenile literature. 2. Gastrointestinal gas—Juvenile
literature. I. Title.
QP121.S82 2009
612.2—dc22
2008033558

Photo research by Tracey Engel

Cover photo: © JUPITER IMAGES/ABLESTOCK/Alamy

The photographs in this book are used by permission and through the courtesy of:
Alamy: Design Pics Inc., 10; blickwinkel, 22; Daniel H. Bailey, 29; Nature Picture Library, 30;
Peter Arnold, Inc., 31; Nigel Cattlin, 35. *Corbis:* Chuck Savage, 25; Envision, 37; Layne Kennedy, 41
(bottom). *Getty Images:* Leroy Simon/Visuals Unlimited, 5; Stone/Howard Kingsnorth, 6; Peter Dazely, 8;
Stone/Brad Wilson, 13; 3DClinic, 16, 33 (bottom); Stone/Stephen Frink, 23;
Clarissa Leahy, 27. *Shutterstock:* Gelpi, 26; Lepas, 33 (top);
Audrey Snider-Bell, 39; Tonis Valing, 41 (top).

Editor: Joy Bean
Publisher: Michelle Bisson
Art Director: Anahid Hamparian
Series Designer: Daniel Roode

Printed in Malaysia

1 3 5 6 4 2

CONTENTS

GASES IN, GASES OUT

Darn it! Your class is late for lunch. By the time you get your food, it's almost time for recess. You scarf down your food and gulp down your milk.

But then something happens. All the air you swallowed while eating your lunch bursts out of your stomach. It rushes up your throat, and there's nothing you can do. A long, loud burp erupts from your mouth. Gross!

Some kids laugh.

Others scrunch their eyebrows and shake their heads.

"Excuse me," you mumble. But it doesn't seem to help.

Swallowing too much air can lead to an embarrassing situation. But air isn't all bad. In fact, you couldn't live without the mixture of invisible gases that makes up air. You'll be amazed at all the ways taking gases in and letting them out makes life better for you—and for other animals, too.

After an insect molts, or sheds its skin, it gulps extra air. This stretches the new outer covering before it hardens so the insect has more room to grow.

When a fish pumps gases into its body it gets lighter and rises toward the water's surface. When it lets gases out, its body gets heavier and sinks.

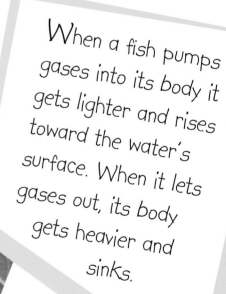

A moth caterpillar stands next to its molted skin.

WHAT A GAS!

Your skin. Your hair. Even your heart and brain. It's easy to think of solid body parts.

You have lots of liquids in your body, too, such as blood and spit and snot.

It's harder to name the gases floating around inside your body. That's because they're usually invisible. But if you pay close attention, you can use your five senses to detect some of them.

- When you inhale, or breathe in, you can see your chest move out. That's because the **lungs** inside your body are filling up with air, just like a balloon.

- Put your hand in front of your nose as you exhale, or breathe out. You'll feel a gust of invisible gases rushing out your nostrils.

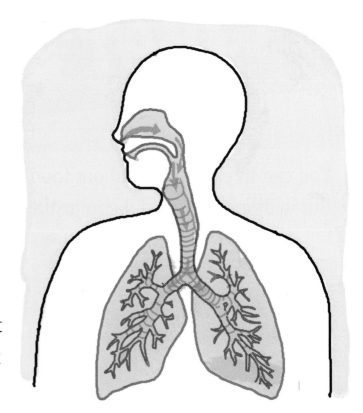

- You know from experience that gases can smell. Just think of your brother's stinky farts. Ew!

  - Farts can be silent, but sometimes you hear loud popping noises as the gases blast out your butt.

    - You usually don't notice the gases floating around inside your mouth, but it's hard to ignore a nasty-tasting burp.

WHAT'S IN AIR?

You can live a month without food and about a week without water. But without air, you'd die in just a few minutes.

Why is air so important? Because it contains **oxygen**. All the cells in your body—that's right, all five trillion of them—need a constant supply of this invisible gas. They use it to release energy from the foods you eat. Energy gives your body the power it needs to live and grow.

Without oxygen, your muscles couldn't move. Your stomach couldn't break down food. And your brain couldn't think. Oxygen isn't the only gas in air, but it's the one you depend on most.

A Remarkable Record

How long can you hold your breath underwater? The next time you go swimming, ask a friend to time you with a stopwatch. Most people can hold their breath for about a minute, but the world record is 15 minutes and 2 seconds. It was set by Tom Sietas of Germany on August 9, 2007.

Gases You Inhale		Gases You Exhale	
Nitrogen	78.62%	Nitrogen	74.90%
Oxygen	20.84%	Oxygen	16.60%
Carbon dioxide	00.04%	Carbon dioxide	5.30%
Other	00.50%	Other	3.20%

AIR ON THE INSIDE

Most of the time, you inhale about 1.6 gallons (6.1 liters) of air a minute. That works out to 96 gallons (363 l) per hour and just over 2,300 gallons (8,706 l) per day. That's a lot of air!

All that air enters your body through your nose and mouth. It passes down a series of tubes inside your neck and chest and finally reaches your lungs.

Your throat, or **pharynx**, is located behind and below your nose and mouth. It opens into your **esophagus**, which carries food to your stomach, and your **larynx**.

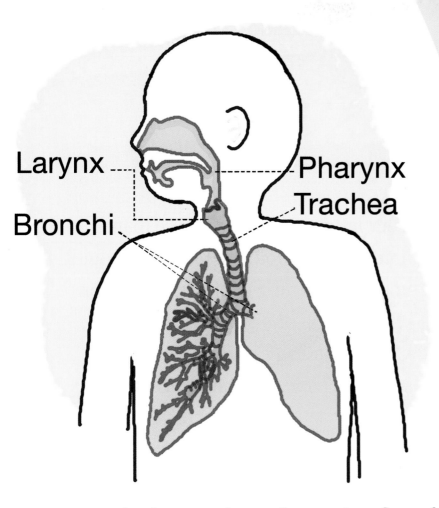

Larynx

Pharynx
Trachea

Bronchi

At the top of your larynx is a flap of tissue called the **epiglottis**. When you swallow, your epiglottis closes, so food heads down your esophagus instead of into your larynx.

Below your larynx is a ridged tube called the windpipe, or **trachea**.

Your trachea branches into two **bronchi**, which enter your lungs.

Pick a Pipe

Ever had food "go down the wrong pipe"? When you swallow too fast, your epiglottis doesn't have time to close. Food enters your larynx and clogs your trachea. Most of the time, a few quick coughs gets your food back on track.

GOOD VIBRATIONS

Your larynx does much more than hold your epiglottis in place. Without it, you couldn't sing or shout, whistle or whisper, sob or sigh. Most important, you couldn't say a word. That's why some people call it the "voice box."

When you exhale, air rushes out of your lungs and up your trachea. As it travels through your larynx, it passes two flaps of tissue called **vocal cords**.

Most of the time the flaps rest along the walls of your larynx. But when you want to use your voice, the flaps stretch across your larynx. As air squeezes through the tiny hole between them, your vocal cords vibrate, or shake, and produce sounds. Your teeth, tongue, and lips work together to convert those sounds into words.

When you yell at your sister, you let out lots of air all at once. But when you giggle at a friend's joke, your breath comes out in short, shallow bursts.

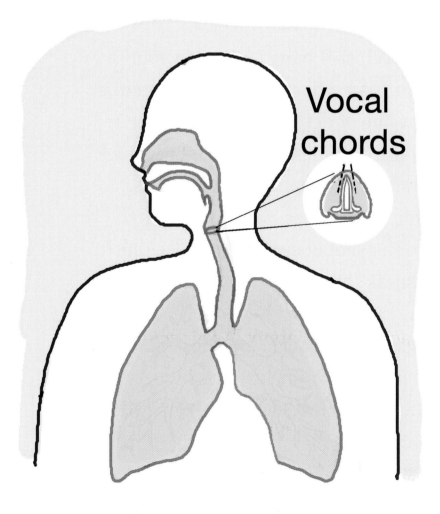

Vocal chords

Long and Low

Men usually have deeper voices than women and children. That's because their bigger bodies have larger larynges and longer vocal cords. The longer the vocal cords are, the less they stretch. And the less they stretch, the lower the sounds they produce.

MUCUS AMONG US

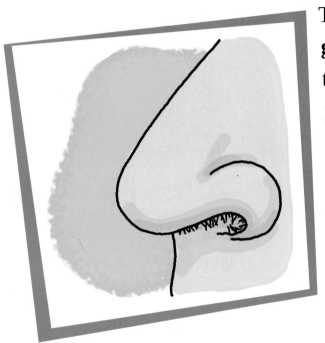

The air you inhale is full of dust, **germs**, and other pesky particles. If they aren't stopped, they can damage your lungs or make you sick.

Small, stiff hairs just inside your nostrils are your **respiratory system**'s first line of defense. They trap the largest particles. Many more get stuck in the slimy snot, or **nasal mucus**, lining your nose.

But snot doesn't stop all the tiny trespassers. Some sneak through your nose and whiz down your pharynx and larynx.

Just like your nose, your trachea and bronchi are constantly cranking out a fresh supply of sticky, icky mucus. The slippery slime traps most of the remaining particles. Then tiny hairs called

When you have a cold, your respiratory system goes into mucus-making overdrive, and your cilia can't keep up. Excess snot drips out your nose. You cough up gooey gobs of mucus and phlegm. Then you swallow them or spit them out.

cilia sweep the mucus and its load of garbage up to your pharynx, so you can swallow it.

Your lungs make mucus, too. This **phlegm** is your body's final weapon against the irritating invaders that threaten your lungs.

A LOOK AT LUNGS

You can't cut open your chest and take a look at your lungs. You'd make a bloody mess. And boy, would it hurt! Luckily, it's easy to imagine what your lungs look like.

Your lungs are spongy sacs about the size of a football. Packed inside, a network of tubes that could stretch from Washington, DC, to Denver, Colorado, holds more than 1 gallon (about 3.8 l) of air.

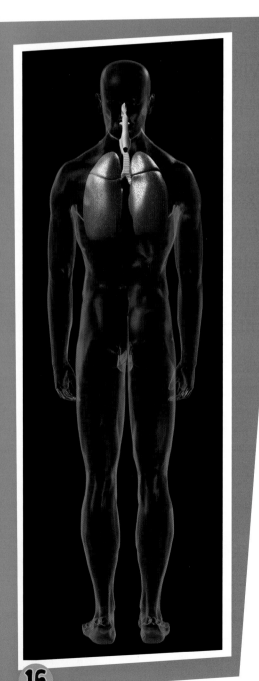

This illustration shows the placement of the lungs in the body.

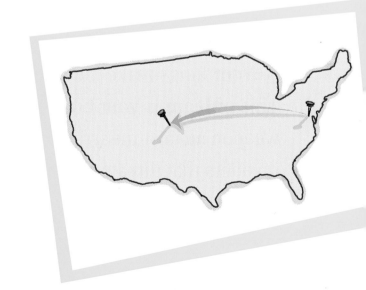

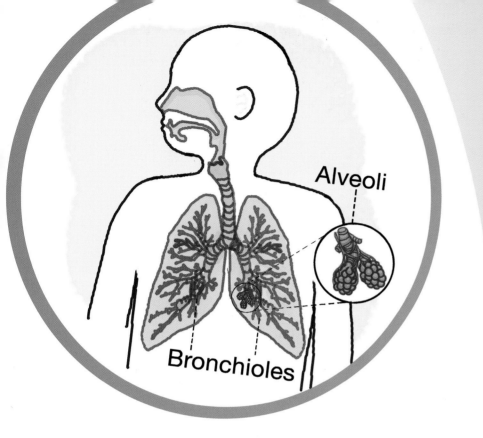

Alveoli

Bronchioles

The pattern of tubes looks like a maple tree tipped on its side. A few large tubes branch off the bronchi. Deeper inside your lungs, the tubes split into smaller and smaller branches until they end in thirty thousand tiny twigs called **bronchioles**.

Instead of leaves, your lungs have about 600 million **alveoli**—tiny clusters of sacs that look like bunches of grapes. If you cut all your alveoli open and stretched them out, they'd cover an area the size of a tennis court.

Peak Performance

No one knows why, but experiments have shown that your lungs work hardest in the late afternoon. Between 4:00 and 5:00 p.m., lungs take in 15 to 20 percent more air than at any other time of day.

ENERGIZE ME!

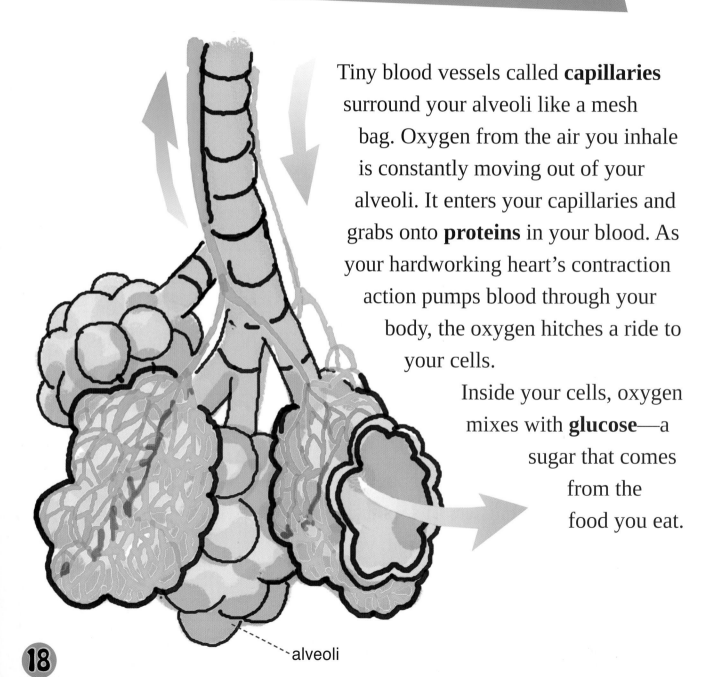

Tiny blood vessels called **capillaries** surround your alveoli like a mesh bag. Oxygen from the air you inhale is constantly moving out of your alveoli. It enters your capillaries and grabs onto **proteins** in your blood. As your hardworking heart's contraction action pumps blood through your body, the oxygen hitches a ride to your cells.

Inside your cells, oxygen mixes with **glucose**—a sugar that comes from the food you eat.

alveoli

This chemical reaction produces all the energy your body needs to live, move, and grow. It also produces water and a gas called **carbon dioxide**.

Your cells can use the water but not the carbon dioxide, so your blood carries it back to your lungs. When you exhale, carbon dioxide rushes through your trachea, larynx, and pharynx. Then it exits your body through your nose and mouth.

Huff, Puff, It's Cloudy Stuff

Most of the water in your body exists as a liquid, but some of it is a gas called water vapor. Every time you exhale, some water vapor escapes. You breathe out about 2 cups (0.5 l) of it every day. Most of the time, water vapor is invisible. But when it hits chilly winter air, it changes into tiny water droplets that form a little cloud.

RESPIRATION CALCULATIONS

Most of the time you breathe, or respire, about twelve times a minute. Each breath delivers about 2 cups (0.5 l) of air to your lungs.

When you play soccer or ride a bike, your body needs extra energy. And that means your cells need extra oxygen. You may end up huffing and puffing up to sixty times a minute. Each gasp delivers as much as 1 gallon (3.8 l) of air to your laboring lungs.

You can check your respiration rate right now. It's easy. Sit quietly in a chair and use a watch with a second hand to count the number of times you breathe in one minute. Your results will be more accurate if you do three trials and then find the average.

Try the same thing after five minutes of walking, five minutes of running in place, and five minutes of doing jumping jacks. Which activity requires the most energy?

How Slow Can They Go?

Some animals have trouble finding food in the winter, so they hibernate. Because their bodies slow down, they need less energy to survive. During hibernation, a dormouse breathes about once a minute. Some hibernating bats can go up to two hours without taking a breath.

GOT GILLS?

Land animals aren't the only creatures that need oxygen to survive. So do sharks and sea stars, trout and tadpoles, octopuses and oysters. But lungs work only in air, so these animals use **gills** to remove oxygen from their watery world.

Gills

A fish gulps oxygen-rich water into its mouth. As the liquid flows over the gills in its pharynx, oxygen enters the fish's blood. Then the fish's tube-shaped heart pumps the blood to all its cells.

Water contains less oxygen than air, so gills have to work hard. Your lungs take in only about 25 percent of the oxygen in air. But some fish can remove 80 percent of the oxygen in water.

Whales and dolphins look like fish, but they're mammals—just like you. Every few minutes they rise to the ocean's surface and inhale air through the blowholes on the tops of their heads.

Back-End Breathing

When a dragonfly hatches, the first thing it does is drop into the water. As it crawls among water plants, it takes in oxygen through gills in its rear end. If an enemy gets too close, the little insect shoots water through its gills, blasting itself out of harm's way.

PULLING AND PUMPING

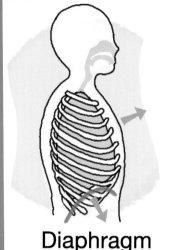

Diaphragm
moves **down**

Most of the time you don't think about breathing. It just happens. That's because your body is always hard at work—even when you're asleep.

Whenever your cells need oxygen, your brain sends a message to the muscles in your chest. Your **diaphragm** drops down, pulling air into your nose and mouth.

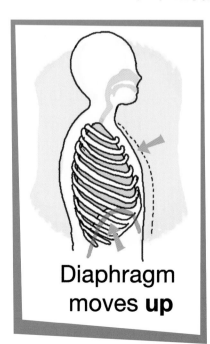

Diaphragm
moves **up**

At the same time, your **intercostal muscles** lift your **ribs** up and out. This makes your chest cavity bigger. Then air rushes into your lungs and blows them up like a pair of balloons.

A few seconds later, your diaphragm relaxes and moves up. Your intercostal muscles push your ribs down and in. This makes your chest cavity smaller. Your lungs collapse, pumping air up and out of your body.

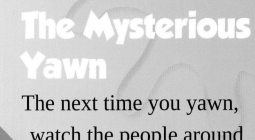

The Mysterious Yawn

The next time you yawn, watch the people around you. Anyone who saw you yawn will probably start yawning, too—but nobody knows why. Most scientists think that people—as well as other animals—yawn when they're tired or bored. They say yawning sends a quick shot of oxygen to the cells. But that doesn't explain why yawning is contagious, so researchers are still looking for answers.

DIAPHRAGM DISTRESS

"Hic, hic." Hiccups are a real pain. They make it hard to talk and hard to eat. And they can really embarrass you in the middle of class.

Most of the time your diaphragm moves in a regular rhythm—smooth and steady, up and down. But that can change if you're nervous or excited, or if you eat too fast or too much. Your diaphragm may jerk and jolt, shudder and shake, causing you to suddenly suck in air. The pressure of that rushing air snaps your vocal cords, producing a "hic."

Some people say you can get rid of hiccups by standing on your head. What do you think? Maybe you should give it a try.

You can try to stop hiccups by holding your breath, drinking from the "wrong side" of a glass, or putting a little sugar on your tongue. But even if these remedies don't work, your hiccups will probably go away in about five minutes.

When Hics Don't Quit

According to the *Guinness Book of World Records*, Charles Osborne of Anthon, Iowa, had the hiccups nonstop for sixty-eight years. They started in 1922, when he was twenty-eight years old, and continued until 1990. For all those years Mr. Osborne hiccupped twenty to forty times a minute. That's more than 430 million hics!

CAN'T SQUELCH THAT BELCH

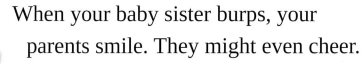

When your baby sister burps, your parents smile. They might even cheer. But that isn't what happens when you let out a good one. Your parents probably scowl, especially if you don't say, "Excuse me."

When you eat, you don't swallow just food. You swallow air, too. If you drink soda with your meal, you're also swallowing carbon dioxide—the gas in all those little, fizzy bubbles.

Normally, the gases you take in travel to your lungs. But when you swallow food, your epiglottis slams shut. So the food—and the gases—end up in your stomach.

After a while your stomach can't hold any more gases. The gases burst out, race up your esophagus, and explode out of your mouth. Buurrp!

You usually belch a few times after you eat, but you'll burp more if you eat too much or too fast, or if you drink through a straw.

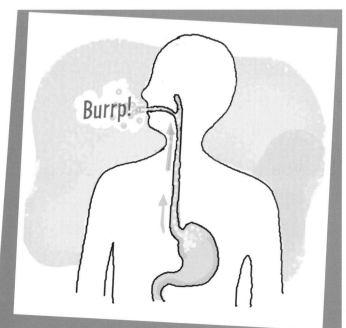

What's That Sound?

Cup one hand, hold it under your opposite armpit, and then pump that arm up and down. What do you hear?

Some people call that nasty noise an "armpit burp." Others say it's an "armpit fart." Either way, it's produced in almost the same way your voice is. As air squeezes through the gap between your hand and your arm, your skin vibrates to make the sound.

THE BEST BELCHERS

Think your friend is the world's best belcher? Think again. An average cow burps two hundred times more gases than a person. Every year North America's cattle belch about 50 million tons of gases into the air. People burp gases such as oxygen, nitrogen, and carbon dioxide. But cattle burp mostly methane, the main ingredient in natural gas. Some people use natural gas to heat their homes. Believe it or not, the methane from ten cows could heat a small house—if only we knew how to collect it.

Cows aren't the only animals that belch **methane**. So do sheep, goats, deer, buffalo, and many other large plant eaters. These **ruminants** have four-part stomachs. It's the first area, the **rumen**, that lets out methane burps.

Rumen

Why do these animals burp so much? Because they can't digest, or break down, grasses. The plants are too tough. But billions of bacteria live in a ruminant's rumen. As the minimicrobes feast on grass, they produce a material that animals can digest—plus lots of methane. That's why ruminants are the world's best belchers.

The Methane Menace

Methane is one of the gases that causes global warming. Scientists are looking for ways to decrease the amount of gases that cows and sheep belch into the air.

RUMBLE, TUMBLE, GROWL, AND GRUMBLE

The classroom is quiet, and everyone is hard at work. Suddenly, you hear a loud, rumbling sound.

Everyone stops what they're doing and looks around.

You look around, too, even though you know exactly where the noise came from—your stomach. You felt it tumble and quake.

Know what the ancient Greeks called a rumbling tummy? *Borborygmi.* They were trying to create a word that sounded like the noise they heard.

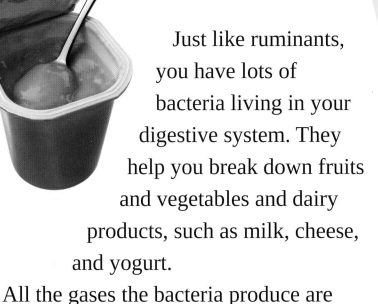

Just like ruminants, you have lots of bacteria living in your digestive system. They help you break down fruits and vegetables and dairy products, such as milk, cheese, and yogurt.

All the gases the bacteria produce are constantly churning and tumbling inside your stomach and intestines. When your digestive system is full, food usually muffles the gassy growling. But when your digestive system is empty, the sound can be loud and embarrassing.

Your intestines sit below your stomach (top right). Your small intestine (center) is surrounded by your large intestine.

A Gaggle of Gases

You don't eat the same kinds of foods as cows and sheep, and you don't have the same kinds of bacteria living in your gut. So even though your bacteria produce some methane, they produce many other gases, too. The most common ones are carbon dioxide and hydrogen.

FART FACTORIES

Pass gas.
Break wind.
Let one rip.
Cut the cheese.
Toot.

Who would have guessed that something as simple as farting could be described in so many ways? After all, it's something everyone does every day.

Some people say boys fart more than girls, but that's not true. Most kids pass wind about fourteen times a day and give off enough gas to fill a 1-liter soda bottle. Where does all that gas come from? The digestive system.

A ruminant burps methane because it spits up the food in its rumen and chews it again and again. Each time the thick, chunky cud comes up, so do the gases produced by bacteria.

But people don't chew cud (thank goodness!). So the gases in your gut keep building up. As food particles move through your stomach and intestines, so do the gases. Finally, they escape as a fart.

Can't Stop the Pop

What causes the popping noises you sometimes hear when you fart? The walls of your **anus**—the hole at the end of your digestive tract—vibrating back and forth. The loudness of the fart depends on how fast the gas rushes out and the tightness of the muscles around your anus.

Goats are ruminants and burp up methane, just like cows.

CLASSES OF GASES

Your farts can contain as many as 250 different gases, but some are more common than others.

About 20 percent of your farts contain mostly nitrogen and oxygen. These gases entered your stomach with your food but weren't released as burps. Nitrogen and oxygen farts can make a lot of noise, but they usually don't smell too bad.

The rest of your farts are made mostly of methane, carbon dioxide, and hydrogen. These gases form as you break down food. They usually aren't too loud, but they're a little bit smelly.

If you've eaten cauliflower, eggs, or meat, you'd better hold your nose. As these foods break down, they produce **hydrogen sulfide**—a gas that really reeks.

Farty Foods

Hard-to-digest foods such as beans, onions, broccoli, and cabbage produce the most gas. Some people have trouble breaking down a natural sugar called lactose. They fart a lot when they eat ice cream or yogurt, or when they drink milk.

A Farting Falsity

Ever heard the saying: "Whoever smelt it, dealt it"? It's not true. The farter usually smells the stench last. Because gas blasts away from the culprit's body, the stinky scent takes a while to reach his or her nose.

FUNCTIONAL FARTS

People aren't the only animals that fart. You might have been unlucky enough to have smelled a dog passing gas. What a stinker!

Who's the biggest tooter in the animal kingdom? It's the elephant. It's a huge animal, and it eats a lot of hard-to-digest plants.

Most animals fart for the same reason we do—to get rid of gases that have built up in their digestive systems. But a few creatures have discovered that farting has some unexpected benefits.

Some snakes hiss when enemies get too close. Others shake their rattling tails. But Sonoran coral snakes and western hook-nose snakes have a different trick. They let out a fart that can be heard from up to 6 feet (1.8 meters) away. That's enough to spoil any predator's appetite!

How do herring find one another after the sun goes down? They fart. The blasting bubbles of gas sound like a high-pitched raspberry as they shoot though the water. Other herring can hear the noise, but larger fish can't.

Farts as Fuel?

A fart is like a miniature rocket engine. If astronauts could have holes in their suits, their farts could propel them through space.

GAS IN THE PAST

Because gases are invisible, we don't pay much attention to them. So you might be surprised to learn about all the roles they play in our bodies. And we aren't alone. They're important for other animals and plants, too. They have been for millions of years.

Plants appeared on Earth long before animals—and it's a good thing. Animals can't survive without them. Animals depend on plants for two things: food and oxygen.

Plants and animals make perfect partners. Animals inhale air, use the oxygen in it, and release the carbon dioxide. Plants use that carbon dioxide—along with water and energy from the sun—to make food. And guess what they give off—that's right, oxygen. How perfect is that?

Fossilized Farts

In 2002 a scientist named Lynn Margulis accidentally dropped and broke a piece of **amber**, or fossilized tree resin, with a 20-million-year-old termite inside. Oops!

Luckily, Margulis turned a mistake into an opportunity. She drilled into tiny bubbles near the termite's body and tested the gases inside. What did she find? Methane and carbon dioxide. The gases were fossilized farts produced by bacteria inside the termite's gut.

alveolus (pl. alveoli)—A rounded structure at the tip of a bronchiole. It is where oxygen passes out of the lungs and into a capillary.

amber—Fossilized tree resin. Resin is a thick, sticky liquid that oozes out of some kinds of plants.

anus—The hole at the end of the digestive tract.

bacterium (pl. bacteria)—A tiny, one-celled living thing that reproduces by dividing. Some bacteria can make you sick.

bronchus (pl. bronchi)—A tube that connects the trachea to one of the lungs.

bronchiole—A tiny tube inside a lung.

capillary—A tiny blood vessel through which oxygen and nutrients move into cells and carbon dioxide moves into the blood.

carbon dioxide—An invisible gas that animals make as they use energy from food.

cilium (pl. cilia)—A tiny hair. Cilia in the respiratory system sweep snot, mucus, and phlegm containing invading particles to the esophagus or mouth.

diaphragm—A sheet of muscles that forms the floor of the chest cavity.

epiglottis—A flap of tissue at the top of the larynx. It closes when you swallow, so food travels down the esophagus to your stomach.

esophagus—The tube that connects the pharynx and the stomach.

digest—To break down food.

germ—A tiny organism or particle that can make you sick.

gill—A body organ that fish and many other animals that live in water use to take in oxygen.

global warming—A worldwide increase in temperature.

glucose—A natural sugar that provides humans and other animals with the energy they need to live, move, and grow.

hydrogen sulfide—A smelly gas found in some farts.

intestine—The part of the digestive system that breaks down food particles and allows nutrients to pass into the blood. It's often divided into the small intestine and large intestine.

intercostal muscle—A muscle located between a pair of ribs.

larynx—The tube that connects the pharynx to the trachea. It contains the vocal cords.

lung—The body organ that delivers oxygen to the bloodstream.

methane—A gas that contributes to global warming; the main ingredient in natural gas.

molt—To shed an old outer covering that is worn out or too small.

nasal mucus—Mucus produced in the nasal cavity; snot.

oxygen—An invisible gas that animals need to live.

pharynx—A tube that connects the nose and mouth to the larynx. It is sometimes called the throat.

phlegm—Mucus produced in the lungs.

protein—A molecule that speeds up chemical reactions, repairs damaged cells, and builds new bones, teeth, hair, muscles, and skin.

respiratory system—The group of body organs that takes in oxygen and gets rid of carbon dioxide.

rib—One of the bones that supports the front of the chest.

rumen—The first stomach chamber a ruminant's food enters.

ruminant— A large, plant-eating mammal with a four-chambered stomach.

swim bladder—A body organ that helps many fish species control their depth in the water.

trachea—The tube that connects the lungs and the throat.

vocal cord—A flap of tissue in the larynx that plays a role in producing the human voice.

A NOTE ON SOURCES

Dear Readers,

All the books in this series have been fun to research and write, but this one had me laughing out loud. Who knew the respiratory and digestive systems could be such a gas?

I started my research by reading sections of textbooks that discuss how we breathe and break down food. They provided lots of great facts, but most of the fun stuff came from other sources, including the *Guinness Book of World Records*. That's how I learned that lungs are most efficient in the late afternoon and that a man from Iowa had the hiccups for sixty-eight years.

Some of the ideas in this book—especially the grossest ones—came from kids I talked to while I was doing research. Without them, I might not have thought to include armpit burps or explain why you can see your breath while you wait for the bus on chilly winter mornings.

My final step was to read articles from scientific journals and speak to scientists involved in the research. These interviews ensure that the book includes the most up-to-date information about why we yawn, why herring fart, and how ruminants' burping contributes to global warming.

— Melissa Stewart

FIND OUT MORE

BOOKS

Solway, Andrew. *The Respiratory System*. Chicago: World Book, Inc., 2007.

Spilsbury, Richard. *What Are Solids, Liquids, and Gases?* Berkeley Heights, NJ: Enslow, 2008.

Taylor-Butler, Christine. *The Respiratory System*. New York: Children's Press, 2007.

WEBSITES

Get Body Smart: The Respiratory System
Text and diagrams give a complete overview of the parts of the respiratory system and how they work in this site.
http://getbodysmart.com/ap/respiratorysystem/menu/menu.html

Kids Health
This site answers just about any question you might have about your body and keeping it healthy.
http://kidshealth.org/kid/

That Explains It!
This site contains all kinds of interesting information about the human body, animals, food, inventions and machines, and more.
http://www.coolquiz.com/trivia/explain/

INDEX

Page numbers in **bold** are illustrations.

ABOUT THE AUTHOR

Melissa Stewart has written everything from board books for preschoolers to magazine articles for adults. She is the award-winning author of more than one hundred books for young readers. She serves on the board of advisors of the Society of Children's Book Writers and Illustrators and is a judge for the American Institute of Physics Children's Science Writing Award. Stewart earned a B.S. in biology from Union College and an M.A. in science journalism from New York University. She lives in Acton, Massachusetts, with her husband, Gerard. To learn more about Stewart, please visit her website: www.melissa-stewart.com.

ABOUT THE ILLUSTRATOR

Janet Hamlin has illustrated many children's books, games, newspapers, and even Harry Potter stuff. She is also a court artist. The Gross and Goofy Body is one of her all-time favorite series, and she now considers herself the factoid queen of bodily functions. She lives and draws in New York and loves it.